Everything Comes and Goes...

Pictorial Essays From the Desert

Thomas Preiss

Everything Comes and Goes...

Pictorial Essays From the Desert

Thomas Preiss

A Peralta Publishing Book

FIRST EDITION

Copyright © 2013-2016 by Thomas Preiss

A Peralta Publishing Book
Tombstone, Arizona

Manufactured in the United States of America
ISBN: 978-0-9798620-5-2

Library of Congress Cataloging in data
0 9 8 7 6 5 4 3 2 1

Dedicated to Mary Lynn

Everything Comes and Goes...

Pictorial Essays
From the Desert

Thomas Preiss

The Passing of Time

I am a keeper of things: Some tangible—like this photograph I took in 1987 for a photography class. Some intangible—like the memory of this corner, and the afternoon I stood there watching time stand still. I took it in the winter sun—it's warmth—and watched it bend the shadows of things that stood above the agricultural plane.

I thought myself uncreative, and the class syllabus intimidated me. But on that afternoon, as I watched shadows and light move time in a northwesterly direction, across the fields of alfalfa and corn, I had become keenly aware of a creative force that moved within. On this corner in 1987, it dawned on me that creativity is solely self-evident. Capturing slices of time, through a photograph, or in an order of words on a clean sheet of paper, makes me a participant in that wellspring of thought and idea—the universal creative force. I knew that my life had something to distill—something that would pass through the elemental filters—becoming tangible to others, while remaining priceless to me. I wonder still what life was lived on that bus, and where in life the turning of that corner took them.

A Farmer's Time

It was quiet. The road at my feet lay cold and still. It was as rural as 'rural' could be—lined endlessly with irrigation canals and dirt access roads. This was farm country—it brought to mind the cycles of life, and the great stories in literature about reaping what one sows.

I thought of these things as the sun and the horizon shaped the outline of a farmer and a tractor on a section of land, grinding their way into a slide of black and white film. Silently the sun's rays illuminated both man and machine, tracking the elements of effort in living a life that generated good things. The farmer worked alone and there, before me, unfolded the transaction between his hands, on the wheel of a tractor, and the hand of God, elucidating hope, faith, and grace upon the fields of a life lived well.

The Well House

I looked deeply into the formation of bumps and indentations on this well house.

It was the abandoned farm field behind the well house though that tugged hard at my senses.

A great, nostalgic longing for the way things might have been, fermented within—the ever-present wish for a normal life in my family's home. Fictional tales are frequently made of longings and wishes, and are better represented by desert tumbleweeds. As I looked on, I wondered about the hands that wrapped the well house in stucco and white paint, and of what family those hands were members. Where did they go? Rarely is the story of an abandoned farm a good one. Greed within a family, or from the march of development run amuck, are how the stories of decaying farms begin and end. The well house called forth sadness in me that was not mine to feel.

I kept looking into the past, and thought of what a farmer is asked to do in reaping what he sows. What was sown in my parent's home, which still stands on a spec of desert north of this well house? What, now removed by some fifty years, could have possibly transpired there that forces me today, to consider it with such sadness?

What I Am Made Of

Effort.

It is all that I have. I must do my best every day. I am blessed to have a skill, and to work the land that has come by way of grace and chance. I know my time is finite. This knowledge ignites inside me, and brings forth my inner life.

In the eyes of others I see their thoughts. They see me trudge and toil. But this is not how God sees me. I occupy a place in the flow of the seasons of God—a part of the magic in life; magic that finds my worth in the spring, when I plant the seeds of my intent—and at harvest time, when I reap what I have sown; when my existence on an Earth that God created, brings forth good things. I am quiet in the cold, and I chug and breathe deeply in the light of the summer sun. I know I am not the fear of others, or the pettiness of jealousy and bitter thoughts—these things have spoiled the world, and leave it light-less in the negatives of time.

A great understanding moves my mechanisms. I can see the clarity of my being, and can behold with all my might its meaning—as I watch the sun set long over the fruits of my labor. I behold my blessed horizon. I can feel the current of an expanding universe moving through my purpose—and my call—to reach for the reasons I am here.

I am grateful to know the cycles in nature. I have faith in the sun rising—in the colors of a morning sky. I have courage, and perseverance, to work throughout the day. I know peace at night—a job well done lays my head to rest—in complete and satisfying exhaustion.

I am loyal to my calling. I honor the time-tested laws of the land I work. I know my boundaries, and am willing to defend what I know is right, and protect what is rightfully mine. I have been given a spirit that is simple and true, and I know that one cannot ask for more in the fulfillment of living.

I know that what is beautiful in the world, is beheld through eyes that have weathered dreadful and despairing times. I understand paradox, and its power to create deep, meaningful, and long-lasting truths.

I know that work affords play—that light and dark would pale without the other. God has given me all of these things to cherish, and hold as possessions—in thin or flush times. I am humbly and graciously satisfied—knowing that I am, because the light of the universe shines on me—and in me—always.

The Passing of Time Part Two

This photo drops fragments of information from above. The silhouetted crop duster reveals a hot summer sun shining brightly upon a lightly-used desert farm road. Dust obscures the horizon.

The road to yesterday presented itself.

It was a road remembered as less strained; less hurried, but was it really? Did the crop duster pilot feel the weight of unpaid bills? Did the truck driver miss his family back home? What was it that made the road to yesterday a better road then what I was on that day? The sky was filled with sentimental grays—the road pulled at my heart—and I longed for who I was when this moment was caught on film—for the quiet moments that could be found on any road crossing another—as desert farm lorries hurled by—and the hum of single engine crop dusters high overhead—droned into distant melodies of youthful day dreams. The sun's hold on a big sky was the adhesive and the thrasher of all I could see.

From cloudless skies, a seasonal sun shined through everything that could be seen. My eyes shut tight, allowing only a sliver of the day into my walking down the road. It was dry, but a canal flooded one side of the road—with its promise of water for crops and refreshment— renewed me. Shade was scarce—found only under the brim of my baseball cap. I found it interesting that the photo does not reveal what season prevailed when the shutter was released.

The picture made me crane my neck up. It took me back to a time when corn, cotton, and cattle reigned.

The road is now moving four lanes of automobile traffic in both directions, and leads to thousands of freshly grown homes, some occupied, most abandoned.

This is a photo of life as memory. Perception, and longing in the heart, beat upon wings to yesterday, while the day ahead is trucked down the road, into the great unknown.

Wheels Turn

The disappearing thought—something all but forgotten save the trigger that takes one back—to a slice of time—marked by light and shadow at its moment of impact into the psyche—the flare and fire of a black and white photograph.

It was a cold, hard morning. The round objects were returning to the earth—each at a different stage in their descent back into organic matter. It struck my visual senses that Mother Earth's recovery of her elements is the all-powerful force. Her gravity is relentless, taking with it most of the energy expended each day just to remain upright—succumbing to its downward decay.

Yet as feet meet the ground, so does the realization that a life, regardless of how it rolls, will some day release its up–down perspective—returning to the elements—where it might find peace from the presentations of anything above the plain of the curving earth. Safe, and sound, the rolling of a purpose-filled existence ended, while the slumber of its seasons began.

The tires were a representation of paradox. On one hand they revealed the end of intention; the end of a life lived well. On the other unfolded the notion of inertia; the shape of a despairing life sitting idle for too long.

Such was life on a desert farm, were both hard work or laziness showed their true form. One would end well—with a head on a pillow at day's end—exhausted but grateful for the seasons and cycles of life—while the other ended poorly—with the mind and heart falling from grace—with hands and feet losing their intent.

In this series of pictures, decay is in the heart of the beholder—more so than beauty or wonder—because the photos reveal to each of us what we fear, not what we believe. Wheels, windows, the thresholds of doors long laid bare in their utility, represent the mechanisms of life, in both the decay and renewing of each. Paradox pulls at our hearts, because it speaks the truth we long to understand. It asks us to place side-by-side what is and what once was—what rolls and what will no longer. Paradox puts simplicity in the recall of days gone by, while adding layer upon layer of complexity in the days at hand, as we long for the wheels of yesterday to turn again. Please, turn again.

A walk through a deserted desert farm calls to the ancient things within us. Whether the farm is alive—growing crops and coughing smoke out of the tail pipes of machines, or is waiting for its ground to break under the spell of bankers, brokers, and urban sprawl, one will feel the cogs of wheels turning—and of life learning—and of a yearning in our hearts for a simpler time in our lives, where the only considerations made, were whether or not the flowers in a garden would survive the coming rain.

What the Road Knows

I stood on the shoulder, and at length looked down a blistering, hushed, desert road. On a Sunday morning, the road was quiet enough for me to hear the mirage of moisture, on the road in the distance, abandon its own efforts to fool my senses. I stared into the horizon above the road for so long that all of what laid before me, met in the middle, at the point of a pin prick, visually so. I snapped the adjacent photo.

I made the effort to look elsewhere, yet each time, found myself drawn again to that point above the road.

The scene offered me parallel imaginings into both the road's past, and it's future. On either side were abandoned farm fields, which had become the hope for other things; the roll of dice; a decision made between a farmer and a spouse—regarding a secure future on a higher plane—leaving the ground to its cadence of restoration.

The road spoke: "The farms have served their purpose," it said. "What lies ahead for the hands that worked these fields can now only be found by their feet upon me. I am the conduit of life evolving. I am the holder of infinite numbers of blessed horizons, for infinite numbers of American dreams. I am what is beyond the moment under foot. I hold the breath of new life as one foot is put in front of another, in pursuit of a life lived well. I no longer wish to carry the old tired tires of rusting combines. I wish to hold the fleet feet of progress. I wish to see all leave the past and look to my future—a point beyond the pin prick of today's perception—beyond the mirage of fears and 'what ifs,' to a time when standing tall, over what has come to pass, I will be seen as the vessel of life—the path that connects one blessed horizon to the next—the steadfast purveyor of grace and design—the highway that holds futures in a straight line, from today to infinity."

I leaned against the truck, and looked down at the soles of my shoes, wondering where the road voice emanated from. I thought it odd that this stretch of broad highway held a different take on its purpose, one different than my perception of it, which was to hear the heartstrings of what used to be. The road had its own idea about where it was headed, not concerned about where it had been. A moulted Diamondback snake skin, caught in the barbed wire fence that ran the length of the road's shoulder, furthered that impression.

Surprised, I returned my gaze to the road, perceiving it as it saw itself. There were four lanes of traffic on each side of a centered double yellow line. Sidewalks, restaurants, red lights, and left turn lanes appeared. I saw intersections claiming lives in auto accidents, and telephone poles holding Christmas decorations. These things, too, became old and abandoned, as demographics and desires for other things changed once more. The buildings that once held commerce and abundance, were only foundations again.

At last, a solitary pot hole, cutting into layer after layer of development, echoed the road's lost longing for a return to the stillness of a farm, and the quiet of old tired tires, rolling rusty combines into blistering, hushed, Sunday morning mirages.

A Father Fading

A guitar plays in the back ground. The minstrel sings of life's lessons—of the sands of time falling between 'hellos' and 'good-byes,'—of those we could have loved—and should have loved, but chose not to. He sings of rolling tumbleweeds brushing clean the footprints of a family. His clear, tenor voice puts to test how each of us could do a better job of loving the circles in our lives, be it through letters, or a moment on the floor with an endeared pet, or what should have been—between two hearts—when love got hard. He sings truthfully that all we hold in life will be left behind, save the love we give. This love will remain, in the form of a wake ever-moving, through space and time, enchanting all that connect to it.

The circles in life, represented in the forms of pipe, tires, and rims in the facing photograph are leaving, moving away from the camera, around the shed and beyond. The weeds show neglect and reflect the chances we have had, to lift the lives of others, fading to gray. They turn away, blending into yesterday, blurred by our own absurd design to deny love to another.

I think of my father. His memory is a deep, unconcealed cut into *what could have been,* in my life. The circles in the photograph echo his presence—one that had already turned to go, around the corner—gone from being within reach—to becoming untouchable through the filter of memory, and the pain of death.

These circle-shapes were among an inventory of long-abandoned farm equipment and housing, anchored by a rock chimney, standing alone among the workings of a culture removed by progress. Next to the chimney, which stood tall over the shed and tires, rose a tree, sprouting right out of the foundation of the former home. I was left with the indelible perception that whatever was right in the home, and whatever was wrong, was now a tree, full of it's own life, standing tall in the summer sun.

After taking the photograph I put some of the ground I stood on, in my hand. I rubbed it between my fingers, and watched it take to the breeze. Some of it was lifted above me—the remainder carried gently back to the ground. I saw in this separating dust, an analogy of what living becomes.

I see no renewal in the photo. I see no effort in changing the course—in not walking away—in learning a lesson now too late to learn.

There is no hope. I see my father leaving—giving me no word of farewell—of how I should live my life. I am no longer bitter. I am sad that the time between taking the photograph so long ago, and of recently writing these words, has brought me no closer to him.

It is no longer about what my father did or did not do. It is now about what I can do to change my perspective of this photograph. There were many things that I could have done, when the wheels rolled, when the weeds were grass, when the shed was useful, and when more than a memory presented itself—not in black and white—leaving not a trace of my father in me—but in full vibrant color, where he would have known the many red shades of my Mary Lynn's hair—or the smell of my infant son's bald head.

Yes, there were many things I could have done for my father. Not denying him my love would have been the best of them.

The Soul

The ground had been wiped clean by the heavy wheels of earth movers and graders. The process of getting ready the sections of land, soon to be developed by giant home building corporations, was quite methodical and perfect, in its ability to sterilize the land from its past, becoming like white, pure, cleaned silk. There was no odor of any kind. It was of a single plane, and plainly one dimensional, with nothing upright that would ruffle the wind, as it rolled effortlessly over it.

I squinted my eyes, blinded by the white light of progress.

Kneeling down to the white-hot ground, the sun's heat, reflected by the color of the soil, was felt on the bridges above my eyes. As the ground grew closer, so did the pull of the horizon—both were perfect and sterile in their presentation of level and dimension—both free of any form of measurement as to its former function or pending utility.

Suddenly, the hypnotizing sequence of white upon sterile, was broken by an object throwing a tiny shadow upon the vast sectioned sameness of the land. Something about the object lent itself to being out of place, or inside out, or perhaps upside down. When that last notion crossed my mind, I was astonished to see a shoe, struggling to keep its footing, above the claim of the earth.

The ground had grabbed it toe first, and had wrestled it over, so that its sole faced the expanse of the universe above it.

One foot in the grave. It is a belief, often stated, that each of us must contend with from the moment of our first breath. I questioned whether a body was attached to it, as the angle for which the photo was taken did nothing to convince me otherwise.

The sole had seen many a mile, and was now being consumed in whole by the relentless laws of gravity, and sequence. One day has followed another, and taken the shoe further into the dust of time, when finally it will be covered by the progression of humanity, and the souls of so much living yet to come.

The Gathering Had Begun

Work was evident in the field.

The morning sun roasted the baled hay. One could see the fragrant air rising—vapors that were first green, then blue, as their elevation changed. The canals were full of water, tumbling over iron gates— water that was siphoned through a ten-inch diameter pipe rising from the ground under my feet. The gusher intrigued me but thoughts of water would come at another time. Before me was heat, produced by a field alive with labor and effort—abundant with a life-sustaining harvest.

The harvest was a product of work and planning. Skilled farmers and large combines yielded a crop befitting the well-executed cycle of planting and reaping—a cycle repeated millions of times, over thousands of years, representing the one thing man has known throughout the millenniums; by putting one foot in front of the other, by putting one hand on a tool, and the other on the design of the season, one could allow his existence to continue, through the baptism and mechanisms of evolution—the great master design of the universe.

A life must contribute. Living must produce. It is the great 'call-to-arms,' that gives each of us an innate knowledge that we do live and breathe—that we are moving through the days and nights of our blessed horizons.

When I walked out on this morning, I smelled the product of farms among the cooler fall temperatures, where the dawn, then dusk, become the distinct break over the lingering summer season. I felt the beginning of the fall, where the need to gather was awakened.

It is in the gathering—when blessings can be counted—when a sense of fortune and serendipity arise— when destiny is imagined and hoped for—where laughter comes from within.

The harvest in the facing photograph puts to use the notion of first things first. When the gathering is complete, a sense of abundance and security moves to the forefront, making the first thing acknowledged during the fall season a sense of well-being. Sleep is achieved easily. Worrisome thoughts and frets do not find there way into the night—only a sense of being able to rest the mind— with hands and feet calloused but okay.

I feel a sense of reprieve, cradled by a hammock in the morning shade of a mesquite tree, with an ice- cold glass of lemonade resting in the palm of my hand—both as tribute to the summer passing. It is done again.

19

Water

I feel a promise from life when I am near it. I hear the gushing refrains of water bounding over rock, in their opposing recitals of life, longing for the earth's offer to live one more day.

I remember the washing it would give my senses, as I slowly let air out of my youth-filled lungs, sinking ever-so-slowly toward the bottom—and safety—from the anti-life on the surface. Looking up, I saw the thin surface bending sunshine, and rebuffing angry words of an abuser. I was safe in its protective immersion around my eyes and ears—around my skin and limbs. It was a still moment between my immediate, liquid world, and the rage found above. Water was the fence—it protected me—never giving into the desires of those who wanted the water to part in front of them.

This photograph asks me to look down. The water bends the light of the sun toward me. Crystal clear and of the earth, it calls my youthful memories forth. I long to fall face first into the joy that would be had there. Cool water, delicious water. Life-giving and sustaining—the womb of my younger days. I am happy to see you again, to remember you, and to again call you my friend, and my protector.

Water is found in all the seasons and in all ritual. Every religion has claimed it as its own. It is the mud of evolution, and the wine of creation, and gives form to what would be an ash-filled world. It is the heart of renewal, and the soul of recreation, and it cleanses my hands and feet—symbols of my life within.

I have fallen into the water and I am fully submersed. I drink wholly, with as wide a mouth as I can muster, gulp after gulp of God's continuing redesign of each new day.

Worthy

In America we can choose to be anything we want, filtered or unfiltered only by the design of our physical, emotional, and spiritual grasp of who we are.

Rebirth pulls from me a notion that a life must fight for, with much effort that which it is destined to become. Fulfilling life's call requires many shedded skins along the way. Transformations ensue—life leaves experience as its wake, which becomes only a foothold for which to push away from. When yesterday has disconnected from the dawn, we are free to reassemble our hopes and inclinations that our unlimited designs suggest we are—and command that we become.

Existence says that we are not limited by the observations of others, but what we see in ourselves. There will always be the exercise of self-acceptance. There will always be the need to forgive the inequities of life, yet most of all, we will need to protect our perception of what we see in the mirror—giving ourselves room to move—and grace to change—those perceptions that will tilt our efforts into dark and forbidding places.

Beauty is not only seen, but felt, and heard, and spoken as well. Beauty does not distract from what encases it. Beauty leaves nothing undone. Beauty—as all things do in this world that add up to anything—emanates from within, and rises forth like a bird in flight, pushed up and out on a rising sky-bound thermal.

Rain tarnishes the metal we are made of. Life can file thin—to a very bitter edge—the points of our lives—breaking our backs, and our hearts, if we let it do so.

But we can muster and we can gather. We can plan and we can utilize the miles we have tilled to date, and see ourselves as God sees us. Movements toward our blessed horizons hone who we are in God's eyes. Godzilla, found in the photograph to the left, is the reflection of us all who have exerted great effort in our lives, to fulfill our intentions, and are now found beautiful and worthy of our place in the morning sun.

Fate

The picture on the left represents fate to me for this reason; the subject of the photo is seemingly Immovable, and forces life and light to move around it, causing shadow and shadow's cousin—death—to follow.

Who and whatever we have become, fate has played its hand. Whether we are shadow or light, black or white, or shades of gray elements that take form, fate has put us exactly where we are today. The objects of the photograph have been brought together; the ground pushes up tumbleweed—the well's siding collects light—the curve bends shadow to a point indiscernible but unique—all of it fleeting as one moment fades into another.

This well is no longer. Fate ended its usefulness. Wells like this one have long fascinated me, even as a child, when my curiosity found me down in the hole, looking up and down lengths of pipe for other sources of light—for crawdads—for whatever was delivered at that moment. I will never forget the smell—like life drying. On a hot summer day the well provided relief. Cold and damp, I'd sit at the bottom, not recognizing the glory of my childhood imagination, as it flowed over the well's rim—a wild assortment of random thoughts, woven together without reserve.

The wells and my boyhood are gone, but certainly not forgotten. Fate has removed me from such things as irrigation wells, but not necessarily boyhood imaginings. I can, as a middle-aged man, still day-dream. I can sit right here, right now, and imagine my feet on the rim, walking, balancing, without fear of falter.

My hands are sturdy, like stilts—pushing my feet high over my head. My eyes dart to the dark, but always present, well bottom—with pipes leading to underground lairs and pots of gold—with water suddenly gushing toward my face, cooling my childish take on the day. The well, known symbolically in an adult world as the spring for every hope, is known to me as a simple challenge for my boyhood abilities. My feet come down into the interior. My nose presses against the cool cement walls, and I examine every inch, perceiving in the gaps and crevices a world of constellations, and the endless shapes of the day ahead.

Fate all-too-often pushes living outside the center of our imaginations. We must not let it pull from us the very things that make life worth living. Imagination is ageless—as is love— and forgiveness—and hope—all wellsprings that can, in the end, outline and shade our adult understanding of fate.

The Rusted "I Love You"

I have made the mistake of saying "I love you," as a way of saying goodbye on the phone. It's become a statement that says "okay, I'm done talking, I have to go, we can talk later, goodbye," rather than communicating that most eloquent of human emotions; love, which states "okay, I believe in you, I trust you, I want to grow old with you, and build a life with you."

I guess I could say all those things on the phone when it's time to say goodbye, and as I write this, I realize that it is just those words that really should be said anyway, all the time, as a continuing commitment to what the phrase "I love you," means to those who speak it, and to those who hear it.

What has lost its luster for me is Valentine's Day. I've made and won the fight in not letting Christmas fade into a commercial joke. I'm not willing to fight for Valentine's Day. I don't need Hallmark to tell me it's time to tell my wife I love her—I can say it better anyway. She does not want me to waste money on flowers, and says that sweets are the manifestation of the devil, designed to ruin her health and girlish figure. Jewelry will always be received well, but economics can hamper such an effort, and fortunately for me, she gets that.

So how I do I tell the one I love, that she is loved? Simplicity always serves me well. It seems that no matter what I do, throughout the year, to tell my wife that I love her, she hears and understands the implications of the expression completely.

On a recent bike ride along the many fences one can find in the desert, and while thinking of a way to tell my wife that I love her, I spied the shape of a heart suspended from a taut line of ancient barbed wire. I unwrapped, then re-wrapped it back into place, making this rusted "I love you," (facing page) for her. I've since given her many of these wire hearts, on many days that cannot be called Valentine's Day, and while the gift itself has no value, the thoughts behind them mean everything to her; I believe in you—I trust you—I want to grow old and build a life with you.

Simplicity throughout the year, versus dead flowers, the devil's cane, and someone else's thoughts on cards one day a year, is working quite well for me. May it work well for you as well.

Ingenuity

Creation. God's call. Man's too. God's claim. Man's aim. The picture shows the ends but not the means. So much of man's ingenuity, with God's designs, went into creating a tire tube. Riding a wave of thought, from points around the world, with one idea chasing another, invention stepped in to culminate in a rubber tube of air.

Changing all life forever, the inner tube increased safety on the road, and saved countless lives in doing so. How many corners did this tube navigate? How many close calls were managed well? How many grand babies have been born because this tube saved the lives of countless grandparents?

With renewed interest, we must all stop taking so much for granted. Fire, rain, inner tubes, compassion—these are all things that must remain as targets of our gratitude. The technology used just to create this page of words is mind-blowing. Hundreds, if not thousands of lives, lives that sparked one bridge of thought to the next, have gone in to the making of this book. With renewed appreciation, I realize centuries old technology found on the blade of the book cutter, compiled with seventy years of discovery within the four walls of Xerox make this book possible. I will also mention the wheels that have turned through time to make available to me the coffee and food I've eaten this morning before writing, giving me the nourishment my mind needs to tap into the creative flow, moving just above my head.

The hand of ingenuity, which is really billions of hands in the ingenuity process, has put me on this office chair with these thoughts, studying an inner tube as it becomes what Mother Nature will make of it again.

Ingenuity makes each minute lived count for something more then a fleeting moment passing. God's claim. Man's aim. Our designs on necessity, our designs by inspiration, our designs in making life worth living, our designs in all the arts, in all engineering, in all philosophy, are represented here by the passing of rubber to dust.

Dug In

Through song and story, living comes and death goes.

We are moved by the sound of the ocean, or the wind between the trees, and we decide where we will go, and what we will do.

Time is clocked by the moon, space is the inspiration for the tune, living emanates brightly about us as the sun keeps warms our sleep, and gives us hope for a better tomorrow. Getting 'dug in,' is not only a house to call home, but a heart that narrows as people, places and things come and go in our lives. Getting dug into a frame of mind that allows the elements to pass is our call in living.

The picture to the right was taken thirty years ago. The sealed-off barrel still sits, slowly yielding to processes too measured and deceptive to ever monitor, and what happens next is our realization that being dug in has buried us.

Living can, if left alone, become decayed bargaining; the same old tune; the same relentless ending, the same expectation at sunset that rises and shocks us awake at night from our sleep.

Its true; the barrel at the right will out-live us. Long after we are gone, it will sit, dug in, too heavy to move, too unwanted to change, too plain to see in color, too inexplicably ingrained in my conscience to ever be useful as inspiration. It is dead heavy, dead silent, dead to use, its shadow no longer useful to its light. I think it ugly. I think I'm bitter. Aging has made me so. My skin, like this barrel, shows pocking. My heart skips when I lunge from my easy chair. I am unfortunately dug into this moment and it is ill omen to me to gaze upon the hard sturdy seams of this metal. Its purpose is obvious; it can be turned into a thousand different things. I am done evolving. I am done in my usefulness. I can level no more land, I can hold no more water.

I can only write my way through. I guess that is something. I am normally not so pessimistic. I think for balance a small display of pettiness, of reality, not of hope, will let me know what I don't want to be in my life; and that is to be like this barrel. I don't want to get dug in.

30

Direction

Where do we go from here? What drives us? Inspiration? Utility? Love? The wind and rain? Gossip? Faith?

Our outlooks drive us. We are what we think. Fear drove me wild at times. By far love has pushed me furthest, and it continues its grace-filled presence in my life. For a brief period, not too many years ago, money had a large hold on me. I once thought money was the direction I wanted to go. There was too big a price associated with that path however. Relying on Wall Street and politicians to hold up their end of any deal became simple stupidity on my part. Moving in the direction of money soon felt like rubber drying in a hot summer sun.

So where then? In the direction of music? In the direction of beauty? Of intellectual stimulation. Of friendship? Of setting example? In the direction of virtue or of sin? It has been written that the road, literally, is the great equalizer, the great teacher of worth as well as frailty. It is understood, out on the road, that both parts are necessary to the development of a soul. The road, and where this old tire has been, has no doubt seen its share of courage and deceit, of loyalty and infidelity, of fear and joy.

We pound out our paths. We beat them mercilessly, hoping to sink our teeth into the American Dream. Yet look at the American Dream. For most it has become an abandoned tire on the side of . . . a road. The options for most have become infinite dots on a horizon. Three years after the abandonment of our American Dream our reality is as satisfying as a nap in the warmth of the sun. We have learned to live without our credit score. Imagine! We don't feel like old, abandoned tires. We are renewed. We are inspired. The rush of a beautiful universe expanding in our lungs and in our thoughts has become our own American Dream. We are products now of love and faith. We see ourselves as so much more than a folding business and a broken mortgage. We are brave. We know the elements of living, and have, by the grace of so many, and so much, embraced our lives as vital, and simple, and beautiful things, perfect as waves, perfect as wind, bare as old abandoned tires, but perfect in our symmetry. We thank the road for giving us our resilient rubber souls, and finding in them all of the great characteristics of living a good life.